All inquiries should be addressed to:
Barron's Educational Series, Inc.
250 Wireless Boulevard
Hauppauge, New York 11788

International Standard Book No. 0-8120-6089-X

Library of Congress Catalog Card No. 88-929

PRINTED IN THE NETHERLANDS
8901   987654321

Marjolein Bastin

VERA THE MOUSE

Vera in the Garden

Translation by Emilie Boon
Verse by Jean Grasso Fitzpatrick

BARRON'S

New York • Toronto

When I find my first buttercup
    I know it's spring.
Oh, isn't it just
    the prettiest thing?
The yellow petals have
    a buttery shine.
In a vase on the table
    it will look just fine!

Then I take out
    all my summer clothes.
Little Doll says
    I'm crazy—who knows?
I must admit,
    it *is* a bit chilly.
Maybe I'm being
    a little silly!

Eveyone's in my wheelbarrow
    going for a ride.
Look how they've all
    squeezed inside!
Afterward, they'll
    use the rake and hoe
To help me make
    the garden grow.

Look how we planted
　　our watercress seed.
Little Doll made a heart
　　because she can't read.
I know my ABCs
　　so I've written my name.
But it will all taste delicious
　　just the same.

A robin's egg fell
    out of its nest today.
Oh, what will Mother
    Robin say?
Let's put it back
    with tender care
Before Mother Robin
    gets a scare.

I like to count ants,
    one by one.
But Chick and Doll
    don't think ants are fun.
They're afraid the ants
    will crawl and creep
All over their paws
    while they're asleep.

Little bird,
    you've sneaked away!
What will your
    poor mother say?
When you've learned to fly,
    you can do anything,
But for now you're going
    under Mama's wing.

Ladybug, this poppy
　　is for you.
It's a beautiful color—
　　and you are, too.
As soon as I saw it,
　　I could tell
It had to be yours
　　'cause it matches so well!

We've decided to take
a little break,
So we've put away
our hoe and rake.
It's very warm
outside today,
And weeding's tiring,
I must say.

See how the violets
    in my garden grow!
They're really putting
    on quite a show.
I'm collecting the violet
    seeds that drop
So next year we'll have
    another crop.

Sunflowers grow
in my garden, too.
Guess who likes them?
The chickadees do.
The seeds must be
their favorite treat.
There's hardly anything
they'd rather eat!

I think Mr. Robin
    looks great, don't you?
See his pants and scarf?
    They're both brand-new.
I knitted them myself,
    to keep him warm and nice
When winter arrives
    with its snow and ice.